Molly Moon's

Hypnotic Holiday

Georgia Byng

WORLD BOOK DAY

specially published for World Book Day 2004
Thursday 4 March 2004
www.worldbookday.com

MACMILLAN CHILDREN'S BOOKS

Also by Georgia Byng

MOLLY MOON'S INCREDIBLE
BOOK OF HYPNOTISM

MOLLY MOON STOPS THE WORLD

Coming in 2005
MOLLY MOON'S HYPNOTIC
TIME TRAVEL ADVENTURE

First published 2004 by Macmillan Children's Books
a division of Macmillan Publishers Limited
20 New Wharf Road, London N1 9RR
Basingstoke and Oxford
www.panmacmillan.com

ISBN 0 330 43747 X

1 3 5 7 9 8 6 4 2

A CIP catalogue record for this book is available from
the British Library.

Printed and bound in Great Britain by Mackays of Chatham plc, Kent

Molly Moon had been in bed with the curtains shut for two days. She wasn't ill with the flu, brought on by the chill November weather. She wasn't sick from eating New York hot dogs. Molly was in bed in the dark because she had hurt her eye.

Her right eye really hurt if she moved it. Of course, moving her *good*, left eye made her bad, right eye move too, so *both* her eyes had been out of action for two days. And she had lain, blind as a mole, with a hospital patch on her damaged eye and a scarf round both, listening to the TV. She felt very sorry for herself, and wished that she had a mother or father to comfort her, which of course she didn't, because she was not only a runaway kid, but an orphan too.

She did have Petula though. Petula was Molly's pet black pug. Poor Petula. She'd sat patiently in the stuffy gloom, waiting as Molly tossed and fidgeted between silk sheets in her emperor-sized bed. For Molly and Petula lived in an extremely grand penthouse suite, on the top floor of New York's luxurious Bellingham Hotel.

Molly had been worrying. Her most scary worry was that she might have damaged the sight in her right eye. Her second concern was a fairly fantastic one. It was a worry that you or I could not have. For Molly's eyes were more than just tools of vision. They were hypnotic.

Hypnosis. This was Molly's special talent. And her closely-set, hypnotic eyes were her first-class ticket in life. With them, she'd travelled to America, made her home in this hotel in Uptown Manhattan and bagged herself a starring role in a Broadway musical called *Stars On Mars*. Molly's dancing style was clodhopping and her voice was as crackly as a piece of burnt bacon, but she had hypnotized every single person at the theatre to believe that she was a sensational new star. If her hypnotic eyes stopped working, things would get a lot more difficult. Really very hard. Really starched.

Starch. Starch is a substance made from potatoes and it is used to make clothes look extra-well-ironed. You can make a piece of material as stiff as a board by spraying lots of starch on to it and then ironing it. This is why restaurants use starch. It makes their napkins crisp and smart. Now, if you are a bit squeamish, you won't like knowing how Molly hurt her eye. But this is how, all the same.

On the night of Molly's eye accident, she and Petula had been dining in a restaurant. A snazzy one with pink tablecloths, called The Flamingo. Both Molly and Petula had been very hungry from a day of hard work rehearsing dances and songs at the theatre. Molly had spent the whole afternoon going over a tap-dance sequence with a giant alien land-squid, who danced very fast. So she was particularly famished.

When the waiter arrived, she ordered a ketchup sandwich and caviar for herself and a bowl of mince for Petula. Then she took the bird-shaped napkin that perched in the crystal goblet in front of her, and innocently gave it a good, sharp, flick-of-the-wrist shake-out. Little did she know that that particular napkin was dangerous. Lethal. It had so much starch drenched through it that its edges, once ironed, had become *razor sharp*.

As Molly flapped the napkin open, its razor edge caught her eye.

If you've ever been stung in the eye, you'll know the agonizing pain that Molly went through. An ambulance was called and she had to go straight to the Manhattan Eye Hospital.

There she was told that she had a small cut in the cornea of her right eye. She was given two different kinds of painkillers, a solution to bathe her eye in, a supply of black eyepatches, and advice – to go to bed for three days.

The first night, Molly had horrible nightmares. She dreamed that she was on the stage at the Manhattan Theatre with five tap-dancing squid. They were circling her, clicking and tapping their green tentacle feet, and the more they danced the more feet there seemed to be. Soon there were hundreds of seaweedy feet pounding around her – far too many feet for Molly to keep up with. She danced hopelessly and woodenly in the middle, until one of the aliens gave a deafening screech.

'Loo-loo-look at her!' he gobbled. 'She's a fa-fa-fake. She can't dance.' In her dream Molly tried to turn her hypnotic gaze on the slimy monster, but when she did she found that her eyes were jammed. As the aliens moved in on her, becoming more and more real, the more Molly's eyes felt dead and useless. Then, terrifyingly, her eyes shut so that she couldn't see at all.

And around her the angry, bubbling voices of alien squid mixed with people from the theatre shouted, 'She's a fake! She's a low down, dirty fake. Send her back to Briersville Orphanage!'

Still with the scarf around her eyes, Molly blindly peeled off the satin duvet and wiggled her skinny, spammy legs. She wrinkled her potato-shaped nose and breathed in the thick, stale smell of the room, which was a mixture of dirty socks, dog and scented orchids from the huge bouquet of get-well flowers send by the producer of *Stars On Mars*. So she couldn't bear being cooped up like a battery chicken any longer and she felt very guilty about Petula. She carefully unwound the scarf from her head, and, slowly, she opened her good eye. She was pleased to find that her bad eye, still under the patch, didn't hurt *quite* so much today when it moved. Cautiously, she looked at the cluttered surface of the bedside table. Every one of the red, danger-zone pills that the doctor had given her had been popped out of its plastic pod. Now she was to take the stage-two purple pills. This was brilliant! It meant she was on the road to recovery. There was no way she was going to take her patch off, but at least she could use her *left* eye. And that meant she could go out.

Going out would be different. Unfortunately Molly would have to behave like a normal child. She wouldn't be able to hypnotize people. She couldn't possibly hypnotize anyone using just one eye. She didn't want to even try it, as, if she dilated her good eye hypnotically, her bad eye, under the patch, would dilate *too*, and then the cut in the eye would surely split again. The idea of this happening made Molly wince. She must take a holiday from hypnotizing. She couldn't possibly risk visiting the theatre. If she met anyone from there she needed to be on top hypnotic form. Instead, she could take Petula out for a walk in Central Park. Perhaps they could visit the zoo.

'I tell you what, Petula,' she said, scrunching her pet's ruckle-furred neck, 'to make it up to you, we'll make today a holiday. How about it? Fancy seeing some sea lions? Maybe we can catch feeding time.'

As Molly heaved herself out of bed, Petula gave an enthusiastic bark and began running around in circles. Then she dived into her basket to recover a stone she'd been sucking.

Molly weaved her way past dim piles of new clothes in tissue paper, tripping over boxes of new shoes that she'd been bought, and stumbled to the window. Bravely she drew back the heavy cream curtains. Hard winter sunlight poured into the room.

Outside, New York sparkled, all steel and glass and stone, its towering skyscrapers standing like a crowd of massive concrete people. Twenty storeys below, the hard tarmac street stretched out to left and right, joining others in the organized American grid-system way. Molly had a bird's-eye view of the roofs of shiny cars as they beetled along.

Molly couldn't be bothered to have a bath. She needed to stretch her legs too badly. So she slipped off her pyjamas and put on her jeans and sweatshirt. She stuffed some dollars into her pocket, found her trainers under the plasma TV screen and her woolly hat in a drawer where the maid had tidied it. She scooped up her room key, and finally began looking for Petula's collar and lead.

She soon found the lead. It was wound around the leg of the balcony table. But the collar was nowhere. Or at least Molly couldn't find it in the messy room. Petula had to be on a lead. She'd be so excited getting outside that she might dart in front of traffic.

Molly hunted for five minutes, then gave up.

'I tell you what, Petula. I can't find your ordinary collar, but since you're going to have a holiday today, I don't see why you shouldn't wear your party necklace.' Molly went to the safe and tapped in her code.

3 0 0 7. (Molly used this code because she thought that a 3 on its side looked like an 'm', the 0s looked like Os and the 7 on its side was almost as good as an 'n'.) With a slinking, electronic noise, the safe opened. Inside were wads of hundred-dollar bills and a flat, velvet box. Molly took out the box and shut the safe door.

She opened the box. Inside it were two things. The first was Petula's fancy collar with four diamonds on it that had been given to her by the rich producer of *Stars On Mars*. Molly leaned over and fastened it around Petula's neck.

'It's a good idea to wear it,' she said. 'If you got run over by a bus and had never worn it, you'd be sorry.' Petula wagged her tail in agreement.

The other object in the box was a present that Molly had bought herself – for a lot of money after she'd won a small-town talent competition.

It was a valuable golden pendulum, and for Molly it was more a souvenir than a hypnotic tool. She wasn't a practised pendulum hypnotizer. Molly couldn't be bothered to go back to the safe. She swung the golden-chained pendulum about her neck.

Stepping out on to the street in her new red leather coat, Molly paused for a moment and let Petula's lead stretch as she went to sniff a fire hydrant.

On the sidewalk opposite the marble-stepped entrance of Molly's hotel sat a familiar figure – a puny young man of about twenty, who lived on the street. He often slept and hung about at this particular spot because there was a grate in the pavement where warm air blew up from the subway station below ground, and because the wealthy guests from the Bellingham, like Molly, sometimes gave him tips. Molly thought of him as the Domino Man, because among his few possessions were a couple of small sacks of dominoes. These he lay out in front of him, inviting passers-by to play. Today a long, orange sports car was parked at the kerb and the slumped Domino Man was listening to a tall, athletic figure, who cast a dark shadow over him. The upright person was waving his arms about as he talked and was gesticulating in a way that showed he liked people to pay him a lot of attention.

Molly whistled to Petula, wound in the stretch lead, and they crossed at the lights. They stopped by a rubbish bin and Molly pretended to read a half-torn advert for the Coney Island Circus that was plastered to its side.

Out of the corner of her good eye, she noticed that the well-dressed, tanned New Yorker had a wallet in his hand. He was fingering a wad of banknotes.

'So,' he was saying heatedly. 'You're suggestin' that I should play you dominoes, even though if *you* win, *you* get the contents of this, but if I win, I get nothin'.'

'You get the pleasure of winnin'. I ain't got much to give ya,' said the tramp, tapping his ripped pockets.

'You're right there. You've got about as much as a trash-heap skunk. An' you look like one. I expect

you've tried to keep a dog but that they've all run
away since you smell so bad.'

'My dog died,' said the tramp.

'Cos ya din't feed it?'

The tramp looked away, then back at the polished
shoes in front of him.

'So you wanna play or not?'

'I'll tell you what I'll do,' said the man, pulling a
pair of black leather gloves out of his coat pocket.
'I'll do a deal with you. If you win, you get the contents of my wallet, as you're suggestin', and you'd
be lucky too, because I won at the casino last
night.'

'But why would you want to risk *all* your money
on a game of dominoes?'

'Because it's not all my money, ratbag, it's like a
drop in the ocean for me. An' I like to gamble. It
gives me a kick. Anyway, you're forgettin' your side
of the bargain. If I win, you pay me back by enter-
tainin' me.'

'And how could I do that?' asked the tramp uncer-
tainly. 'I'm no comedian.'

'I know that. I can see you're a complete loser.
You've got about as much talent as a cockroach. The
way you can entertain me is by streakin'.'

'Streakin'?'

'Yeah, by takin' all ya clothes off an' runnin'
around in ya birthday suit until some ol' lady tells ya
she's gonna call the cops.'

'But I'll get booked.'

The suited New Yorker looked impatient. 'An'
after the ol' lady or whoever has screamed or

whatever, you can jump in that fountain there an'
have a bath. Cos, I'm tellin' ya, you stink. That's
what I get if I win.'

'And that's what you call entertainment?' The
tramp stared incredulously at the man above him,
and then, hungrily, he eyed his wallet. The embar-
rassment was worth risking. Making his decision, he
gathered the dominoes up in a rag sack and offered
it up.

'Take your pick. Fifteen each.'

And so the charged game began. Molly edged
closer and was soon their audience. Neither really
noticed her as both were intent on winning.

One by one the black bits of wood, with their
white blobs, began to snake across the dirty pavement. The rich guy was doing well for a while and
then, to Molly's delight, Lady Luck seemed to turn
her eyes on the tramp. Suddenly the wealthy man
had four goes in a row when he didn't have the right
dominoes. Four times he was forced to take another
domino from the bag. With each setback his temper
rose. The tramp looked up apologetically as he rid
himself of his last domino. He'd won. The man
above him still had eight to lose.

Neither man spoke. For a moment the rich guy
was rigid with fury. Then he relaxed. Balletically,
and with a malicious twinkle in his eye, he stretched
his right leg out and poked a domino with the toe of
his shoe. He flipped another forward by giving it a
delicate kick.

'We never shook you know.' Then he turned
towards his car.

Molly was amazed. Open-mouthed she glanced from the poor-as-a-pebble tramp back to the city boy. There was no way that he ought to get away with this. She glanced about to see whether any other passer-by had seen the injustice. But the street was full of people caught up in their own worlds, rushing to work.

Lost for help, Molly glanced back at the hotel and wondered whether the doorman could sort the situation out, but he was occupied, carrying a trunk into the building. Then she thought of calling a New York cop, but a second later she realized that this idea was ludicrous. She'd be laughed at. Yet this was no laughing matter. The Domino Man had just been cheated out of money he'd won fair and square. He needed that money! Molly hesitated.

This was nothing to do with her, she said to herself. Today was supposed to be a holiday-have-fun day, not a good-deed day. But she was feeling furious at the meanness and the unfairness. All sorts of memories of her own past, when people had treated her badly, flooded through her. How she would have *loved* a fairy godmother figure to suddenly appear and sort the situation out. She could be the Domino Man's fairy godneighbour. (After all they were neighbours). But would she be able to hypnotize the rich man?

Molly *did* know of other ways to hypnotize people without using her eyes. One was by using her voice alone. This was how she had succeeded in hypnotizing her very first subject, the old trout-faced cook at the orphanage. But she was very out of practice. The other way was by using her pendulum. Molly had only done this once before.

It could all go very wrong. Even if it worked, wouldn't she then have to hypnotise the tramp too? Molly didn't have long to debate pros and cons in her head, because the sports-car driver was finding his keys. On impulse, she stepped towards him.

Molly's pendulum was a beautiful object made of solid gold and etched with a black spiral that wound its way into its centre. She held it out and let it drop down on its chain.

'Excuse me, sir, I was wondering whether you'd like to buy this for, er, ten dollars. It's worth a fortune,' she began. 'Perhaps, if you look at it, you'll see just how special it is, and you'll feel lucky.'

The young man looked at the pendulum, then confusedly at the patch-eyed, pirate kid before him.

'It's worth a fortune,' repeated Molly. 'As you look at it now, you'll – start to see – its value. Look into – the spiral.' Molly's left eye was throbbing hypnotically, urging her to use its power on this man, but she forbade herself to use it – she'd already decided that she didn't want to risk her right eye's surface splitting again. So, instead, concentrating as hard as she could, she began to swing the pendulum gently from side to side. Inside, she wondered whether this would work.

'Look into – its spiral,' she chanted, 'Just look – See – You'll see – how valuable – the pendant – is, if you – look.'

'What are you?' scoffed the man. 'A peddling gypsy?' For a moment Molly thought she'd lost him, but then, she noticed, he wasn't taking his eyes away from the pendulum.

Molly was thrilled, but she was determined not to let this distract her. She now turned her hypnotic tone up and swung the pendulum ever so slightly more.

'Look right into the spiral,' she suggested. 'You'll see – and you'll feel more – relaxed. Unwind your – mind. Travel the – spiral. And you'll forget – what has – happened to – you here – you'll feel calm – and warm – and the swinging – spiral will draw – you in – Right in – that's right – until you are – there, in the centre – of the spiral.'

The man's eyes were now fixed. Molly could see the spiral reflected in his pupils. She felt the time was right to nail him.

'In and in – keep looking – until you are – completely – and utterly – under – my – power.'

Radiating warm waves now rose up through Molly, starting at her toes and flowing through her veins. It was the fusion feeling – the fuzzy feeling that let Molly know that someone was hypnotized. It fizzed through her like hot froth. The pendulum had worked! This was wonderful! The golden disc caught the sunlight and seemed to give her a friendly wink. Molly loved the heady feeling of having someone under her power. Suddenly now the idea of taking a holiday from hypnotism as well as her theatre work seemed absurd. Hypnosis was in Molly's blood, just like acrobatics is in the blood of a circus tumbler.

The city slicker stood in front of her, as still as a

sentry awaiting orders. And, since he was such a schmuck, *what* orders she was going to give him! Before she and Petula finally left for the zoo for their day-off treat, she wanted to rearrange him a bit.

'Right, mister,' she said in a stern tone, 'I'm afraid today is going to be a little uncomfortable for you, so hold on to your hat.'

Looking worried, the hypnotized man reached up for an imaginary cap.

'Because of the rude way you treated this man, and because of the, er . . .' She couldn't think of the word for a moment. Then it came to her: 'Because of the *dishonourable* way you backed out of paying up, I've decided that today you should learn a lesson.' Molly glanced at the straggly haired tramp. Then she smiled.

'In a minute,' she said, 'you're going to follow me into the hotel opposite. There you will swap your clothes with this, um, gentleman here. You will think that the deal you made was to give him, not just the contents of your wallet, but the contents of your *life* for the day. Whilst he is discovering what it's like being *you*, you will be here, finding out what it's like being *him*. And you will think about how horrid it must have been for him to meet a jumped-up jerk like you.'

At this point the young man sitting on the pavement began to object.

'Excuse me, I d-don't think you should do this. If I'm not mistaken, you've just, just hypnotized this guy. I didn't do a deal where I got the contents of his life. No siree.'

'Listen,' said Molly. 'This is the guy who just told you you smelt like a garbage skunk, and that you had as much talent as a cockroach.'

As she scrutinized the tramp's dirty, unsure face she realized he obviously had a very low opinion of himself. It suddenly struck her that it might be very gratifying to really help someone using hypnosis. So far, she'd only really helped herself. This was an amazing opportunity. So, with charity in her heart, Molly decided then and there to drop her plans of a holiday completely. She would devote today to helping the unfortunate Domino Man improve his life. She could use her pendulum if she needed to. Petula wouldn't mind.

'You,' she said, reaching down and giving the scruffy man a hand up, 'you are in desperate need of some confidence building. Your self-esteem is so low that you don't even know what confidence is. You shouldn't have let this twit insult you like he did. So, today, since I've got nothing better to do, and since my confidence used to be the size of a ladybird's handbag but it isn't any more, today we're going to sort you out.'

'We are?'

'We most certainly are,' said Molly.

'But you can't just go around rearranging things like you're suggestin',' the tramp objected. 'If you start the dominoes knocking each other over like this, who knows what will happen!'

Molly wondered what he was talking about – as far as she could see the dominoes were laid out on the pavement.

'Trust me,' she said, smiling. 'This is going to be brilliant.'

And whistling for Petula, who was investigating the tramp's rucksack, she wound in her lead and took the two young men by the hand and led them across the street.

'So what's your name?' Molly asked as they climbed the Bellingham's front steps.

'Maximillion Most.'

'Not you.'

The tramp realized with a shock that he was being asked a question.

'Er, well, it's . . . um . . .'

'Um?'

'No, it's, um, Willy. Willy Dumfry.'

'Hmm.' Molly nodded wisely. 'I expect that name was the start of your problems.'

Two hours later, the trio, plus Petula, emerged from the grand hotel. The tanned man with the glossy black hair was now wearing dirty jeans, two thick matted jumpers and the rough oilskin jacket that had belonged to the other. The homeless man was washed and shaved, and smelling of citrus bath oil. The knots in his hair had been cut out by the hotel's hairdresser and Molly had deloused him. She'd often had lice herself (as ninety-nine per cent of people have), so she was an expert at getting rid of them. She'd flushed the seventy-eight bugs down the plughole. They were now swimming around in the pipes beneath the hotel, trying to find a warm, hairy creature to live on.

Even though Willy was too thin for the muscly man's clothes, he was the right height for them, so with the aid of a piece of hidden string the suit just looked a bit baggy. And cleaned up, Molly thought, he wasn't bad-looking. Without his beard, it was now possible to see the bony shape of his face. His nose was a bit on the pointy side, but he had deep-blue eyes and these made his face attractive.

Willy was feeling as if he were in a dream. He hadn't had a bath for weeks. And he'd never worn clothes of such expensive, soft fabrics, nor such comfortable shoes. Molly was surprised that he hadn't asked her one question about how she lived in the Bellingham, or how she'd hypnotized Maximillion Most. She realized his confidence was so low that he didn't even feel he had the right to ask questions. As she chewed this thought over, she led the two men over to the wooden domino ribbon. A few of its bricks had blown up the street, but otherwise it was still there.

'We'll see you tomorrow morning,' she told Maximillion. 'Until then, you will be Willy. Good luck. If you need a bath, there's always the fountain. Remember? – You suggested Willy here should jump in it. It's a bit cold and is full of pigeon droppings, so don't put your head under.'

The tanned, shaven tramp nodded obediently and sat down on the pavement. Petula smelt his shoes.

'Right, Willy,' Molly said to her new pupil as they walked towards the orange Lamborghini sports car. 'The first lesson today is this: You are you, and you have the right to call yourself what you like. If you don't like your name, change it. If your parents gave you a name that has the wrong, er, ring to it, you have a right to bin it. What would you like to be called?'

'Um, I don't know.' Molly gave him a few moments to think and tugged at Petula's lead.

'You could go for Will or Bill. You can think about that for starters.' Petula trotted towards them. 'But for today your new name is Maximillion. Today you are going to experiment with being Maximillion Most.' Molly reached into the new Maximillion's top pocket and felt around for the real Maximillion's wallet. She pulled it out and plucked out a couple of credit cards. 'Today these are yours. And this is your diary.' Molly handed Willy a small black book. 'I think you'd better look inside it to see what you're supposed to be doing.'

The pretend Max looked nervously about.

'I'm not sure if I should be doing this. I mean I can't just kidnap this guy's personality for the day. It's not right. Besides, people in his life will realize I'm not him.' Molly was impressed. At least he was objecting.

'I think the way you should look at it,' said Molly, 'is as a day of medicine for him as well as for you. He needs a strong dose of what he's about to get and so do you. Leave the problems to me. All you have to do is pretend the diary is yours. Come on, look inside.'

Guiltily Willy flicked through the fine, thinly papered pages of the diary, looking for the date.

'Monday the twenty-fourth of November,' Molly reminded him, realizing that living on the streets he probably didn't have much need of the date.

'Here it is.'

'What does it say?'

'It says Cloud Studios, Wooster Street, Stephanie Woolcracker. Listen, I'm not sure about this, I mean who knows *what* he's got planned.'

Molly turned towards the man by the wall and shouted, 'What's your job, that is most days except today?'

'I'm – a – model,' he replied.

Suddenly the way he posed, with his shoulder jutting forward as he talked, made sense. He was a nasty, self-satisfied fellow, but he was also, Molly realized now, good-looking enough to be a model.

For a moment Molly faltered. She gave her prodigy a quick once up, once down. Doubt almost bit her, but then she remembered how ugly and useless she had once felt, before she'd found hypnotism, and she was inspired by the challenge. Reaching into the tailored jacket again, she found car keys.

'OK, buster. What are we waiting for? Can you drive?'

Willy nodded his head faintly and swivelled to look at the fiery orange beast that sat waiting for them at the kerb.

'See, so you do have talent!' said Molly.

'Most people drive in America.'

'I don't. Come on, let's go.'

Soon Molly, Petula and Willy were settled in the pink suede seats of the Italian sports car, looking out at the world passing by through tinted orange glass. Willy cautiously turned on the ignition and the car bounced forwards in three mechanical lurches. Petula's nose hit the dashboard.

'Sorry, sorry, it's just I haven't driven for four years. The last car I drove was a pickup truck . . .' Willy gripped the wheel determinedly and then, white knuckled, they proceeded shakily along Madison Avenue.

'That model's weird,' said Molly, picking up some sunglasses. 'I mean, I like the colour orange – my favourite drink is orange squash concentrate, but this guy's crazy about orange. His car's orange, the windows are orange, even his shades have got orange lenses.' Molly rifled around in the glove compartment and looked at the real Max's things. He had three portable mirrors in there, a shaver, a badge that said in red 'I'm too good for my body', a bottle of cologne, an orange lipstick, some diarrhoea pills, a powder compact, a camera film pot full of nail clippings – 'YUCK! What does he keep these for?' –

a stash of photographs of himself, some mints called 'Minteasers', a few CDs and some more money. Molly pressed the horn, and sure enough the car gave out a fabulous pressurized 'BAAAARPP' noise. Willy swerved.

Molly pushed the button on the CD player. Suddenly the car was booming with a voice that sang, '*I'm number one baby, yeah I am, I'm superman.*'

Willy turned the volume down.

'I'm not sure this is right,' he said nervously for the seventh time, narrowly missing the back of a stall selling bagels. Molly stared up through the sunroof at the clouds above. She hoped Willy would take the day by its horns instead of worrying all the time. '*I'm number one baby, yeah I am, I'm superman,*' sang the voice on the CD.

'This music really isn't me,' Willy went on. 'I mean, I'm about as number one as a *minus* million, and I'm as similar to superman as a penguin is similar to a . . . a . . . an eagle.'

Molly took a deep breath. She realized that the reason why Willy was worrying was because his confidence was so low that he didn't think he even had the right to *pretend* to be superman, even for a short car journey. And that, she realized, was pretty bad.

'Right Mr Minus Million, if that's what you think you are', she declared. '*You* have got to do some mind acrobatics. And the only way to quickly sort you out is to make you think differently about yourself. Stop the car.'

Willy did as he was told and the Lamborghini screeched to a halt.

'What you gonna do? Hypnotize me like you did Max the Most?'

'No. *But* you *are* going to be hypnotized, in a way. You're going to hypnotize yourself. Ever heard of that saying that some people chant over and over to themselves in the morning that goes, 'Every day in every way I get better and better and better . . . ?'

'Yeah, I heard of that.'

'Well, that is an old saying that was actually originally made up way back in 1915 by a famous French man called Emile Coue. It's a *self-hypnotic* saying. If you think about it, of course it is. It's "Positive Affirmation", that's what Mr Coue called it. If you say it over and over, eventually you *do* get better and better and better.' Molly turned to face her pupil full in the face. 'And so today you are going to start doing some Positive Affirmation. You are going to start rubbing out those negative things you think about yourself. You are going to reprogramme yourself.'

'But I'm not a computer. How am I going to do that?'

'For starters you are *really* going to start calling yourself Maximillion Most, because that is the complete opposite to being Minus Million, which you *mustn't* think you are. And you are going to do what this Most guy obviously does, which is to start telling yourself that you are number one. Over and over again that you *are* superman. OK, Maximillion Most? So, repeat after me, "I am number one."'

Willy looked suspiciously at Molly.

'Go on,' she urged. 'Try it. It can't hurt you – can it?'

Willy looked very reluctant and then, as disgustedly as if he'd just pushed a slug up his nose, he muttered slowly, 'I am number one.'

'Good. Now say, "I am superman."'

In the background the voice of the singer echoed Molly's words.

'This is stupid,' Willy objected, wrinkling his nose as if an earwig was crawling around in there. But when Molly frowned at him, he did as she asked.

'I am superman,' he uttered quietly.

'Now say them together.'

The new Max paused, then he gave in. 'I am number one. I am superman.'

'Great.'

As he drove off, although he didn't realize it, he was pushing ever so slightly harder on the accelerator.

By the time they arrived at Wooster Street, Willy was saying his 'number one superman' thing about as loudly as number thirty-two on the volume control of a CD player.

The amazing thing was that the more he said it the better he felt.

However, when they parked the orange Lamborghini in the ivied, cobbled forecourt of Cloud Studios, he began to feel like an intruder and a fake. In one fell swoop the idea of going to the real Maximillion Most's modelling appointment undermined all his positivism and made him feel as warty as a toad.

'It's all right for you,' he said to Molly as his eyes darted about for an excuse not to go in. 'I mean you can just watch, whereas I have to stand in front of the cameras. Can't I just do some of the other bits of Most's day and forget the modelling?'

'Listen, Willy,' nodded Molly, patting his back, 'I told you this was going to be like medicine. Lots of medicine tastes bad. You're just going to have to grin and bear it.' Molly rang the bell on the entryphone.

'I've come to see Stephanie Woolcracker,' she said. Then, 'Come on Max, trust me.'

So, the thin, uncertain man followed Molly and Petula up the grey stairs of the studio building to the first floor.

Inside, the studio was white and bright. It had a huge, vaulted ceiling with skylights in it, and a giant roll of white paper the size of a carpet rolled down from the wall halfway across the room. Two people were standing on the far side. One was a chubby man in black flares and high-heeled boots who was running a steam iron over some clothes on hangers, another was a woman who stood beside a mirrored dressing table armed with a brush and a palette of make-up. At a table on the other side of the room, a skirted photographic assistant was putting film into a camera.

From behind the roll of white paper a smoky voice shouted bossily, 'Come round here.'

Stephanie Woolcracker had a peculiar face – her unchanging expression was a stern one that seemed to suggest she had swallowed a live eel and was trying not to vomit it up again. When she saw Molly and the new Max, she looked perplexed.

'Who are you? I was expecting Maximillion Most.'

'You've got, er, Mickey More instead,' said Molly quickly.

Stephanie Woolcracker didn't look convinced, so to be safe Molly got her pendulum out.

'Have you ever seen one of these?' she whispered. 'It's a pendant with a camera in it.'

'R-really?' said Stephanie Woolcracker, too curious not to look at the pendulum. 'A camera? That's astounding! But how does it work and where's the lens?'

'The lens is right in the middle of the spiral. If you look, you'll see.' In two minutes, the photographer was limp as a damp biscuit.

'So, this is Maximillion Most,' Molly told her.

'OK – whatever you say.'

'What happens next?' Molly asked.

'Zacko,' explained Stephanie Woolcracker, her eyes now with a glazed sheen to them, 'Zacko here – will – dress Maximillion, and Bamby – here will do – his hair and make-up – and then – Ling will shine the – lights and – lastly, I'll – shoot.'

Within a few moments everything was under way.

Bamby, Ling and Zacko eyed the pretend Maximillion suspiciously, but no one complained about him because Stephanie was in charge. Zacko did what he'd been employed to do. He whisked the pretend Max behind a curtain and redressed him.

'Stephie, darling,' he said as he pulled the curtain back, 'the clothes are all a bit big on Maxi here.'

Willy stepped sheepishly out from behind the curtain, dressed in drooping black and white, stripy lurex trousers and a matching sleeveless top.

'I'm like a zebra with a saggy skin,' he hissed to Molly.

'Oh, Zacko, just improvise will – you?' Stephanie suggested in a halting voice. 'We've got – to get – the pictures.'

So whilst Bamby tweaked his hair, making it spiky with gel, and whilst Willy looked pleadingly at Molly, begging her to let him off, Zacko pinned the clothes so they were tighter.

'Are you sure you've done this before?' asked Bamby, as Willy shied away from her powder brush for the fifth time. 'I'm not going to skewer you with this you know.'

As Bamby went to fetch a special glitter from her make-up bag, Molly turned Willy's rotating chair around. His spiky hair made him look as if he had been struck by lightning.

'Right,' whispered Molly. 'I'm going to give you another lesson in hypnosis, so listen. There's another hypnotic thing you should know about. You've heard of charm?' Willy nodded. 'Good. Well, charm is very similar to hypnotism. It really is. Charming people is a bit like charming snakes. If you just turn your charm on, you'll be surprised how it makes people warm to you. They'll be sort of hypnotized by you. Try it.'

'But, but I've never charmed anyone in my life. I don't know how to do it,' croaked Willy, 'I'm about as charming as a . . . as that mould people get between their toes.'

'What, athlete's foot?'

Willy nodded sadly.

For a moment Molly was flummoxed. She'd never really thought about how exactly to charm people. The truth was, she'd never been that good at it herself. She'd just seen other people do it. That's how she knew it worked. But, as she thought about it, she realized there were lots of ways to charm people.

'If you make them laugh you'll charm them,' she began.

'I'm not very funny,' said the new Max grumpily.

'You must know *some* jokes.'

Max thought hard.

'Or I tell you what, you can flatter them. It works best if you mean it though. Just notice something good about each of them and let it slip out naturally when you're talking to them. Or charm them by asking them each an interesting question about themselves. They'll be touched that you bothered to ask.'

So that was exactly what Willy did.

First he dragged a joke up from the back of his mind. It was the one that went, 'Why did the boy wear a nappy to the party?' No one knew the answer.

'Ooh, tell us,' said Zacko. 'Go on, crack our ribs.'

'Because he didn't want to be a party-pooper!'

Molly was the only one who laughed.

'Eeuuurgh, lavatorial! Disgusting!' complained Bamby.

Zacko wrinkled his nose as though he'd smelt a rotten potato. None of them even smiled. Not giving up, Willy tried some charm. He asked Bamby whether she ever painted, since the way she held her make-up brush reminded him of an artist he'd once seen on TV. He asked Zacko if he'd ever been a model himself. He admired Ling, saying how clever she was to know how much light would look good in the photograph. Soon their looks of uncertainty had peeled away.

Standing on the white-paper backdrop and blinking in front of the spotlights, Willy felt as small and vulnerable as a striped bacterium under a magnifying glass. But with Molly smiling at him and mouthing, 'I am number one. I am superman,' he felt bolstered. And he did his best to follow Stephanie's directions.

First he had to hold up a painted, polystyrene rock.

'Try to look as though it's really heavy,' said Stephanie.

Willy put on a face that looked to Molly as though he had a bad stomach ache.

'You look – wonderful. So – strong,' said Stephanie.

Next Willy had to change into neon-pink cycling shorts and have his bony white chest powdered. He was asked to hold up a bicycle that hung from the ceiling from invisible wires *whilst* eating a four-scoop-high strawberry ice cream in a cone.

'Try not to get it all round your mouth like that,' said Bamby.

As the minutes ticked by, Willy found out something amazing. By just deciding not to be embarrassed, and by pretending to be a world-class model, he found himself slipping into the shoes of a professional.

'Fan – tas – tic,' said the doped Stephanie as she clicked away. 'You've got – natural – style. You're looking great. Great. Lovely – darling.' Molly hoped Stephanie could still take good pictures when she was hypnotized.

CLICK CLICK CLICK went her huge black camera.

'You're amaaaaazing!' said Zacko, flicking his quiff of blond fringe excitedly and wiggling his bottom as if he'd never seen such talent.

After twenty rolls of film had been taken, Willy stepped out of the light.

'Phew.'

'I can't wait to see the pictures,' smiled Molly. Then, 'What are the pictures for?' she asked.

'They're for this – year's advertising campaign – for Steel Dream – Works,' said Stephanie, batting her eyelids four times.

'What's that?'

'It's a big American – chain of – gyms, where men – go and – work out.'

'Work out? You mean like doing weights and stuff?'

'Yes,' slurred Stephanie. 'The pictures – are to get – people to come – to exercise – at Steel – Dream Works.'

'But I don't have muscles,' the new Max pointed out.

'No, you don't have – muscles,' Stephanie agreed.

'But aren't your pictures supposed to be of someone who looks like, well like a gladiator – all strong and muscly?'

'Yes, that – was – the idea,' said Stephanie, completely oblivious to the fact that she was heading for trouble.

'So you've taken completely the wrong sort of pictures?'

As if the new Max had asked her whether the world was round, Stephanie replied, 'Yes.'

'Oh,' said Molly. 'Oh. Oh dear.'

Because of her, she realized, this woman Stephanie was probably about to lose her job. Even though she was sour as an unripe apple, Stephanie didn't deserve to be fired. Molly panicked. She dragged Max behind the screen.

'What are we going to do, Max?'

'What do you mean what are we going to do? This was all your idea, Molly. I told you that once you knock the dominoes, they all start to fall over.'

Molly didn't like this. Everything suddenly felt more chaotic than she wanted it to. She ran to the window. Outside there were lots of people on the street. She frantically scanned their sizes and shapes to see whether any of them could fit the Steel Dream Works bill.

'I'll be back in a second,' she said, and she rushed out of the studio.

Petula bounded after her. As Molly skipped down the last three steps to street level, she bumped into an old lady who tripped sideways into her elderly friend. As he was jogged, a loaf of bread fell out of the top of his brown shopping bag and landed in the gutter. Bump, trip, jog, tip, splash.

'Watch where you're going, young lady,' he scolded her. 'Do you think I want gutter-water soup all over my bread?' Molly retrieved the packet.

'I'm really sorry,' she apologized. The two pensioners walked off grumbling and Molly scanned the street. Willy had been right. The domino effect did exist, and by hypnotizing him she had started a chain reaction. She should try and put it right as soon as possible. She must find a better model. Spotting a large man looking into a cafe on the other side of the road, she walked keenly towards him, but as he turned she saw that his face was covered with a spiderweb tattoo. His image probably wasn't what Steel Dream Works wanted. A little brawny decorator wearing an overall came out of the cafe carrying a sandwich. He wouldn't do either. He was too wiry. A muscly grimy-faced man sitting on his motorbike, eating a doughnut was just too mean-faced.

Then Molly saw her saviour. Standing by a street lamp about fifteen paving stones away, adjusting his belt buckle, was a well-built man in blue. His profile looked good. With relief, Molly walked towards him. But as she got closer, he put on his hat and she realized he was a New York cop. She faltered. Her hands began to sweat. Molly had never hypnotized someone with a gun.

Still, she'd got Woolcracker in a fix, so she had to make amends, and right now the policeman was the only suitable model on the street.

She didn't think she should hypnotize him using her pendulum, as it was probably a crime to put a policeman into a trance and someone would see. She would have to rely on her hypnotic voice. It was a long time since she had tried to use it. She took a deep breath.

'Er, excuse me,' Molly began, and she tried to think of something that would take a long time to explain. The cop had skin the colour of demerara sugar and luckily that gave her some inspiration.

So, calming herself, Molly levelled her voice and craned her neck so that she was looking straight into the policeman's eyes.

'Have you ever thought,' she observed expressionlessly, 'how many different shades of skin there are?' She had the man's attention. Now she spoke more slowly. 'There are,' she went on, 'probably hundreds, maybe even – thousands, ranging from – the darkest – almost blue-black – skin, to skin – that is so white

that – it reminds me of – the surface – of the moon.'
Inside her head Molly's voice sounded like a droning machine.

The policeman looked at Molly with interest, wondering what had caused her outburst. He scanned the street to see whether there were other children watching this patch-eyed kid complete a dare. There weren't, and so, because he was amused, he nodded and smiled. Besides, he suddenly felt lazy – lazy as a donkey in the sun.

'I mean,' Molly pushed on, speaking flatly but raising her voice slightly and curling it around some of the words that came out of her mouth. 'I – mean – if – you – think – *think* – deeply – now – right – down – in – the – bottom – of – your – *mind* – calmly – you'll – see – you're – not – really – black – you're – more – cara – *mel* – like – the – colour – of – a – brown – leather – *chair* – you – could – sleep – on – sleep – on – when – you're – relaxed – or – brown – like – the – soft – barky – *hole* – that – a – hiber – nating – dormouse – sleeps – *sleeps* – in – and – I'm – not – really – *white* – I'm – more – the – colour – of – a – pillow – on – a – soft – *bed* – where – you – relax – pinky – white – like – a – mushroom – *room mush* – soft – and – velvety . . .' She paused for a second, impressed that her speech was having the desired effect on the policeman. He looked like he was nodding off. Feeling the moment had come, Molly began to talk him into a trance. 'We're – all – the – same – underneath – underneath – our – skins – underneath – we – all – *relax* – in – the – same – the – same – way – way – down – we – all – *relax* –

when – way – way – down – inside – we – feel – completely – and – utterly – in – a – *trance* – and – now – you – are – completely – under – my – power – and – when – I – click -my – fingers – you – will – act – normally – and – follow – me – and – do – *everything* – I – bid – you.'

And the warm fusion feeling flooded through Molly, showing her that she had complete control. The cop smiled as contentedly as a bee in honeycomb, and Molly clicked her fingers.

Petula barked as if impressed. The diamonds on her collar flashed as if in agreement.

'Thanks, Petula, I think so too,' said Molly, and to the policeman she added, 'Now, er, sir, if you'd please follow me . . .'

In the grey stairwell inside the building Molly briefed her new subject.

'And,' she added, 'you will put your gun somewhere safe. When the job is done, you can go back down to the street and carry on being a policeman. Today, you are going to be the new face of Steel Dream Works, and so you'll show them all your muscles and stuff. You have got muscles, haven't you?'

'Yeees,' the policeman said, flexing his right biceps.

'Stephanie, here's your new model,' she said. 'He's easily good-looking enough to be the face of Steel Dream Works, isn't he?'

Stephanie Woolcracker looked up from the camera lens she was polishing. And then something horrible happened. As if the eel that Molly had imagined in her throat was real, Stephanie Woolcracker opened her mouth and in all its ugliness, the imaginary eel spoke, then disappeared down into her gullet again.

'But he's black,' she said.

For a moment Molly was confused. 'So?'

'So, I don't – like – taking pictures of black people.' The eel now looked like it was wriggling around inside her, as if it was trying to come up again for air.

'Stephanie, you are revolting,' said Molly.

'Some people are like that. I had a man spit on me once because I wasn't Chinese,' said Willy, who had his baggy suit back on. Then he whispered, 'If I were you I'd hypnotize that out of her.'

'You're darn right I will,' Molly declared and, walking straight up to the Woolcracker, she ordered harshly, 'Come with me.'

Behind the paper backdrop, Molly gave Stephanie some life-improving instructions.

'OK. From now on, Woolcracker, if ever you think stupid thoughts like the one you just had when you saw this model, you will moo like a cow. Do you understand? And *each time* you moo you will realize that all skin colours are as good as each other and that the people inside those skins are all the same – human. Also, you will stop making that horrible face where you look like you've swallowed an eel.' Immediately Stephanie Woolcracker's expression relaxed. 'Moooooooooooo,' she moaned as they returned to the others.

'Are you all right,' asked Zacko. But Stephanie Woolcracker already had a chain of new thoughts whizzing through her head and she oozed to the policeman, 'Mooooooo – Darling – welcome. You're perfect for this job. Thank you for coming. Come on, let's shoot. Zacko, dress this man.'

When the policeman stepped out from behind the curtain, in the zebra gym outfit, with his great bumpy biceps glistening from where Bamby had oiled them, he really did look the part. He looked *better* than Maximillion Most would have done. As he stepped into the lights, beaming like a superstar, Molly leaned towards Willy.

'See, sometimes the domino effect *does* have good results.' Willy nodded. 'Now,' continued Molly, 'are there any more appointments in Mr Model's diary?'

The new Max smiled and opened the little black book.

'Nothing,' he said.

'OK,' said Molly, 'well, how about some lunch?'

Willy, Molly and Petula left the flashing studio.

As they passed the biker, who was still sitting astride his motorbike, eating another doughnut, Willy asked Molly, 'I hope you don't mind me being nosy, but what have you done to your eye?'

'I've cut my cornea,' explained Molly. Willy

winced. 'It's nearly better,' Molly assured him. 'I've got some purple pills.'

'Hmm,' hummed Willy. 'I wonder, have you ever tried herbal remedies? I had a really bad eye once and these pills made from wolf-berries healed it real fast. Before we have lunch, why don't we slide into that drug store and get you some?'

'How do I know it won't make it worse?' Molly said nervously. Still, they made their way over the road to a chemist. Molly left Petula outside, sniffing at an empty box. Inside she bought a box of wolf-berry tablets and took a dose.

Just as she swallowed the little sugary pill, she heard Petula bark.

Molly froze. Petula's bark was not the happy-go-lucky one she normally gave when she was excited. This bark was a cry for help. Something horrible was happening to her. Molly rushed outside. She leaped down the four steps of the chemist. Petula barked again and Molly saw her face. But only for a moment, because in the next second, her head was pushed down and she was squashed into the travel box on the back of the doughnut-man's motorbike.

As he revved his machine and skidded away, Molly screamed. Then she frantically searched for someone to help.

'Police! Help!' she cried. 'Someone help! That man has stolen my DOG!'

But the street was unpoliced. People glanced at Molly as if she were mad. A few turned their eyes to watch the bike turning the corner at the end of the street and at its puffs of exhaust that were disappearing into the air.

Willy was now standing beside Molly.

'Did that guy just take your dawg?'

'Yes, oh, this is the *worst*! And there's no policeman to chase him – oh, this is *a nightmare*, this can't be happening! Why would someone just snatch her like that – what does he want to *do* with her?' Molly was becoming quite hysterical. Suddenly she grabbed Willy's arm and pulled him with all her might towards the orange Lamborghini.

'OK, Will, don't ask any questions, don't say you won't. Don't be a coward, don't be slow . . . *just get in the car now and as if your life depended on it, please, drive*!'

Molly rammed her hand in his pocket and found the car keys and shoved him into the driving seat.

'Turn it on,' she shouted. With a roar the engine was ready and in a moment, Molly and Willy were hot on the tail of the smoke-spewing motorbike.

'Do we, do we have to do this?' asked Willy, trembling again.

'What are you talking about?' said Molly. 'Petula is in that box, with the lid shut, like a coffin. I don't believe it! If that policeman wasn't upstairs showing off his muscles, this wouldn't have happened.'

'So, you mean it's your fault.'

'You don't need to tell me – the domino effect and all that – I know. But, Will, this isn't a time to blame me. It's a time for you to really show what you're made of. You've *got* to catch him. Petula needs you to be a real hero – a *real* one. Drive, Will, drive.'

So Willy drove, and took his task very seriously. Out of the corner of her eye, Molly could see his mouth moving ever so slightly. Inside his head, Willy was saying his new mantra. 'I am superman. I am superman.'

The car lurched sideways again and skidded through three lanes of traffic to keep up with the bike.

'But why would a Manhattan biker want Petula?' Molly asked, almost crying. 'Black pugs are rare but not *that* rare. I love Petula more than anything, but why would *he* want her?'

'Hmm,' mused Willy as he turned at a light. 'Maybe the guy thought those diamonds on that collar of hers were real.'

'They were!'

'They were?'

Suddenly everything was clear. Molly felt like a simpleton for not realizing before how attractive Petula's diamonds would be to a thief. Of course they would be. They were worth thousands and thousands of dollars!

After driving for six hectic, tense minutes, wondering how far away the thief was planning to go and keeping a safe distance from him, Molly and Willy followed the slowing bike round a corner.

The biker parked halfway down a scruffy street, opposite a shop displaying wigs and beside a store that sold materials. This was the Garment District. He jumped off his machine and in three movements had opened the metal box on his bike, gathered up a struggling Petula and reached inside his leather jeans for the front-door keys to the huge apartment block before him.

The orange Lamborghini was still moving, but Molly began to open her door. She realized that if they were going to get inside the building too, she'd have to jam her foot in the front door before its latch closed. So, jumping out, she began running down the pavement. The next few moments were slow motion in Molly's mind. The door seemed impossibly far away.

Inside the building, still with adrenalin pumping through him from the thrill of the robbery and still with his helmet on, the biker strode into the lift and pressed the button for the eighteenth floor. The lift doors slid shut. He laughed to himself as he remembered the screams of the rich kid who obviously owned the spoilt pug. He sneered as he thought how ridiculous it was to dress a dog in diamonds. Holding Petula still, and pushing his helmet back so that he could see better, he re-examined her collar.

Below him at the building's entrance, the air device that stopped the front door slamming let out a final QUISH noise as it allowed the catch of the lock to meet its socket. Molly had never run so fast. Then a tall, thin figure sprinted past her. Willy dived at the door, stretching his fingers out so that they slid in between the door and its frame.

'OUCH! That's the first time I've intentionally slammed my fingers in a door!'

'Thanks, Will!' Molly said, breathing heavily as she arrived. 'You're brilliant!'

'Now what?'

Molly peered into the lobby at the stairs and the lift entrance. She watched the numbers lighting up above it. The biker was arriving at the top floor. She stepped inside.

'We can't just follow him up. He might have a gun,' warned Willy.

'Come on, Will.'

'But I'm not Will, I'm Willy.' Will was so nervous that he farted.

Molly screwed up her face. 'OK, for *that* you have to come in with me.' Molly's mind was whirring. If they could get upstairs, then hopefully Petula would be almost saved. Would she? Would Molly's pendulum work on a suspicious, guilty thief? Or her hypnotic voice, would that work? She turned to Willy. She could see she was going to have to give him some more encouragement.

'Will. Let's remember something. Today you're stretching yourself. It's like what actors do when they're experimenting with a part. Today you are playing a part. And right now you are going to *pretend* to be really, really brave and this is going to show you how much courage you *really have* inside you already.'

'Gee, Molly, you've got some weird ways of doing things. I told you about the domino effect. Just look what's happened. This might end up real, real, *real* bad.'

'Listen,' Molly said firmly. 'Sometimes in life you've got to take a risk. Don't be so negative. Maybe the day will turn out good. Besides, if we don't rescue Petula I don't know what I'll do. Today was supposed to be a holiday for her and just look how it's turned out. Think how she must be feeling! You've got to help.'

Willy glanced at the car outside. 'Well, you've done a lot for me today, Molly, so I'll trust you. Just one more time.' With that he started to put his arms up in the air as if he were putting on an invisible pullover.

'What are you doing?'

'I'm dressing myself in courage.'

'Well, if it works for you, fine, but don't do that one in front of other people,' advised Molly. 'Not everyone's as open-minded as me.'

The lift arrived.

With every floor the lift passed, Molly's belief that they were doing the right thing wilted a bit. By the time they got to the eighteenth floor, she was ready to go down again. But the thought of Petula pulled her out. Willy followed.

They stepped into a white, gloss-painted passage. At the end of it was a door to an apartment and to the side was a set of steps that led, it seemed, to the roof. The door to outside was open and treacly Bronx accents floated on the air.

Molly crept up the steps and, as a shy tortoise

might, poked her head out to see what was going on. Willy breathed down her neck.

The rooftop was in a spectacular setting. Molly could see that only a few buildings away was the upper part of the Empire State Building, with its fan-patterned metal top. Around them was a panoramic view of skyscrapers jostling as they shot up into the Manhattan sky. Some went up forty floors higher than the apartment block Molly was in, their sheer sides of windows and glass reflecting a silver sky. Others were the same height. Many of the rooftops were crowned with green water towers. The thief's apartment-block rooftop was set out like a garden, although not a very well-kept garden. It had big pots growing grasses and weeds. Bits of worn-out, half-rotten furniture lay about on its splintered, sun-bleached decking. In the centre was a huge, raised concrete platform with a water tower on top. This was a cylinder the size of a caravan, big enough to carry the thousands of gallons of water needed by all the apartments in the block below. It had a green, pitched roof on top to keep the water inside it clean.

Standing on the platform around the water tower were eight people, all in their twenties. There were three women and five men. Each one was dressed in black leather and, even though it was freezing, four were wearing sleeveless jackets, as if they were so tough that they didn't feel the cold. Their bare arms were decorated with tattoos. Most of them were studded in one way or another. With nose studs, ear studs, cheek studs and, when one made a face at another, Molly saw, tongue studs. The women looked like they had jewellery shops in their ears. One of the men even had bolts set into his head like horns. They were all crowding round the biker.

'Oooer, I don't like the look of those guys,' Willy whimpered. 'They look like the type that go crazy, Molly. Like wolves on the night of a full moon. Dangerous.'

Molly ignored him. With horror she watched the scene by the water tower. The biker had his back to her. The horned man, a fat woman and an ugly guy peered greedily at whatever he was showing them. It was, no doubt, Petula and her collar.

Suddenly, one of the men, who had a peroxide skinhead, opened the hatch of the water tower, and for no apparent reason he stripped off his leather jerkin and his boots, and stepped through. There was a huge, muffled splash causing peels of laughter from the two slim women in the gang. The one in long black boots ran up the steps and poked her head through the hatch. The show-off was swimming around in the cylindrical water tower, screeching and shouting as if he were having a dip in the Arctic Ocean.

Molly chose this moment of distraction to nip across the roof terrace to hide behind a giant urn.

From here, she climbed around the back of the water tower platform and up to the level of the grubby group. Hidden behind a ragged holly bush, she could now see Petula. And Petula, who now caught the scent of Molly, looked up at her, wide-eyed and frightened. She tried to loosen herself from the biker's grip. She barked at Molly to come to get her. Molly didn't know what to do. Right now she was powerless. But she tried to send comforting thoughts to Petula, thinking, I *will* get you out of this mess. I will Petula. I promise.

Molly was furious to see how badly the biker was handling her. His gloved hands were scooped roughly under her stomach as if she were a stuffed toy that had no feelings. She could also now clearly hear their conversation.

The man in the water was called Choker. He was already cold and keen to come out.

'Come on, pull me out. I'm freezing my butt off in 'ere.'

'I tell you what,' suggested the short, ugly, fat man who stood next to the biker. 'Let's shut the hatch.'

'You dare an' I'll kill you, DT.'

'Get yourself out of there, you crazy moron,' said the big-bosomed lady, leaning into the water tower.

'I told you, Doris, I *can't* get out,' shouted Choker.

'Oh, for Pete's sake.' Big Doris leaned over and put her arm in. With the strength of a lion she pulled Choker out as easily as if he were a kindergarten kid.

'That'll teach ya to show off to the ladies,' said a wiry man whose arm was in a bandage.

Choker pushed angrily past him to go down to his apartment to dry off. Molly wondered where Willy was and looked frantically about for him. She hoped he wasn't about to come face to face with Choker.

'So, Flip,' said Doris, stroking the biker's head. 'You've done well. These diamonds should be worth a few bucks. Take the collar off and let me look at it.'

'My mom used to wear a collar,' commented the man with the horns coming out of his temples. ''Cept hers had spikes on it.'

'Ah, ain't that sweet,' said Doris.

She sat down on an overturned crate whilst Flip struggled to get Petula's collar off. One of the skinny women, who had a cigarette clenched between her teeth, held Petula still. As a column of hot grey ash fell on Petula's black fur, she yelped.

'Ah shut up, you uptown bitch.' The woman thought this pun was very funny and began chortling with laughter. 'Get it?' she asked Flip. 'A female dog's a bitch. Get it?'

Molly's stomach turned. How she was going to hypnotize this ugly bunch, she didn't know.

Suddenly Doris yelled, 'Oooh, Cobra baby, come to mama!'

For a moment, Molly thought she was about to see a toddler stepping towards the fat woman, but then she realized that Cobra was far more likely to be a grown man, unless of course Cobra was a pet snake. Molly shrunk behind the bush. Then her heart stopped.

'Had to let him out,' explained Choker, now with a towel round his neck. 'He needed to go.'

As Molly caught glimpses of different parts of Cobra, his large red mouth packed with teeth, his monster body, his panther-sized paws, she realized that what they had there was a Dobermann. And, just as fast, Cobra was calculating in the smell department of his doggy brain that what he had there was another dog, and a new human. He could smell a small spaniel or pug and a young human girl. He bounded towards Petula, but was grabbed by the horned man.

'Oh no you don't. Not yet. Not until we've got her collar off.'

Frustratedly, Cobra quietened down. Now, distracted by the other new scent, he raised his head and began to sniff the air more. Molly looked frantically around for Will. She realized now that he'd split. Run off! She couldn't believe it. So much for dressing himself in courage! Still, what could Molly expect? Willy wasn't superman by any stretch of the imagination. A second later the killer dog was barking.

'What ya barkin' at, honey?' Doris asked him, looking towards the ledge of the water tower. 'Oh, ya silly dawg. I'm gonna take ya to the park soon. You're going stir crazy livin' up here. There's nothin' there, honey.'

But Cobra continued to bark and then to jump so keenly that the horned man could hardly restrain him. By this time everyone's attention was on him.

'What is it, Cobie? A puddy cat? Go get the puddy cat, Cobie.'

Molly shrunk back. In a second, Cobra would get hysterical with curiosity. She didn't want to end up as Cobra's dinner. So, without any more hesitation, she stood up.

The gang were immediately silenced. Molly stood before them, dressed in her red leather coat, with the black patch over her eye and her hair wild as a banshee's. Each one was stunned for a moment. But their quiet didn't last for long. Choker took three large strides up on to the platform, picked up Molly and threw her to DT, who caught her and tossed her so that she landed at Doris's feet. Molly grazed her hands.

Petula began to bark, but everyone ignored her, including Cobra. He growled at Molly.

'An' who in the devil's name have we here?' said Doris sinisterly.

From her unseemly position on the floor, Molly now realized two undeniable truths. The first was that this gang most definitely lived in a state of boredom. The second was that, to them, Molly was a plaything. Molly felt like a mouse surrounded by eight nasty cats.

'The li'l pirate lady ought to learn herself some manners,' drawled Doris, her lips curling playfully.

Molly was completely defenceless. Her pendulum and hypnotic voice were no use to her now. Choker scooped her up as if she were a carcass of meat.

'My oh my, what fine clothes we have on,' he taunted her. 'All the better to swim in!'

With a lunge, he threw Molly into the water tower.

For a second, Molly's world went black, and very, very cold. Icy water shot up her nose. It was above her and below her. It filled her ears. It drenched her clothes through to her skin, her hair through to her scalp.

Then she surfaced. Spluttering, she found her bearings. She felt like she was treading water in a huge teapot.

A shaft of light was coming through the trapdoor entrance, but this was half blocked by Choker. He was pointing and laughing his head off, as if seeing Molly being half drowned in the icy water was one of the funniest things he'd ever seen. Molly spat out a mouthful of water. As she grew accustomed to the light, she undid her coat and with great difficulty pulled it off. She wiped her wet hair away from her face and tried to think straight. Her eye patch had come off and was floating in the water in front of her. The eye bandage had come off too. Molly kept her bad eye shut whilst her teeth chattered horribly. Her legs were going numb, but she had no desire to climb back out into the lion's den above. She might be nearly frozen in the water, but at least she was safe. Then she thought of Petula and the fierce Dobermann and she frantically began to look for a way of climbing out.

Outside, the other members of the gang gathered to have a look at Molly. And, as if she were a joke-telling goldfish, they peered into the dark container and laughed.

Finally Doris said, 'OK, Choker, pull her out or she'll need antifreeze.'

Choker's thick arm dangled into the tower, as welcome as a rope ladder.

Molly stood beside the water tower, shivering and dripping like a sopping kitten. To her left, Petula, now collarless, cowered behind two heavy terracotta pots, just out of reach of the nasty Dobermann, who barked and scrabbled to get at her.

The gang stood in a line, examining her as if she were a performing artist from a freak show.

Then it happened.

There was an almighty screeching noise and Molly saw what looked like a skinny, suit-wearing superman flying through the air. Willy, carrying two heavy sacks of compost, had thrown himself off the ledge above. He landed on the back of Choker, who fell forwards, knocking the tall girl in front of him. The impact was so great, that she lurched violently sideways into Flip, pushing him over. He was winded and knocked into the woman with the long black boots. She toppled and fell on the ground, letting out a deep-throated cry as she branded herself with her hot cigarette. It was a very spectacular illustration of the domino effect! In three seconds, four of the gang were sprawling helplessly on the ground. Willy was dazed. Then, as he saw the outcome of his daring gesture, an ecstatic expression crossed his face.

Doris scowled at Molly and Cobra growled. How

Molly wished she could perform pendulum or voice hypnosis on them! But she couldn't. Voice hypnosis would need time, and she didn't have that. Pendulum hypnosis would be impossible as Doris was far too angry and, besides, the other members of the gang would see, and even if it worked on Doris it then wouldn't work on them.

'So,' said Doris, her lardy cheeks twitching. 'You ain't some kinda one-eyed pirate kid. It was all an act to make ya look cool. Where did ya get your accomplice from? I can see he likes flying. Tonight we'll take him to the Brooklyn Bridge and see how he'd like to jump off *that*.'

Molly was so scared that she couldn't feel the cold any more – fear had exploded inside her and now burned like a nuclear furnace. She and Willy would certainly *drown* if they were thrown into the river under the Brooklyn Bridge. Molly studied the woman's fat face as it contorted and rippled with malice, and blinked as she tried not to faint. And, as she did, she suddenly realized that without noticing it she had opened her bad eye and was using it. She could see through it!

Molly's mind leapfrogged. Did that mean she could now use it hypnotically too? Molly wasn't sure. She knew wobbling movements happened in her eyes when she hypnotized people. Those movements might be bad for her cornea. If it *re*-split, she would be blinded again by that terrible pain. But Molly must take a risk. Otherwise maybe she, Willy and Petula would end up dead. If she'd ever really needed to use her hypnotic eyes, this moment was it.

Taking a deep breath, and concentrating on a beer can by her feet, she switched the hypnotic part of her eyes on. In a few seconds, her eyes were throbbing with the energy inside them.

'What are ya lookin' at, midge?' Doris snarled. 'Look at me while I'm speakin' to ya.' Molly looked up. Her eyes penetrated Doris's, locking on to her mascara-coated pinholes and fixing them in a green, hypnotic glare. Like metal discs tugged by a magnet, Doris's beady eyes were drawn and pulled and stuck. And in a few seconds, she was completely zoned in. She was as powerless as an engine drained of fuel.

Molly realized that they'd be all right now.

As easily as if she were going around popping balls into hoops, she stepped up to each New Yorker and zapped them to Kingdom Trance. With each shot of hypnotism a hot expanse of fusion feeling rose through her. Willy wiped his eyes in disbelief. He marvelled as he watched each confused gang member step up to Molly, only to be struck dumb by her staring eyes. It was fantastic. One by one they stood stiff as snowmen under the icy sky.

Finally, Cobra rolled over on to his back. Molly breathed a sigh of satisfaction and relief. She would tell her hypnotized subjects what to do later. Right now, she had far more important things to do. She opened her arms and Petula bounced out of her hole, rushing up to Molly to lick her on the face.

'You are amazing,' Willy said, watching Molly roll about on the deck with Petula. 'I keep thinkin' I might be dreamin'.' He plucked the diamond-studded collar from Doris's talons.

Molly cuddled Petula and looked up.

'Well,' she said, shivering, 'I've done hypnotizing like this before, so it's not actually as amazing as it seems.' She paused and then a huge grin spread across her face. 'But you.' Molly now got so excited that she shouted. 'BUT YOU . . . YOU ARE A DIFFERENT KETTLE OF FISH. YOU REALLY ARE AMAZING!' Petula barked for joy and Molly jumped up and slapped Willy on the shoulder. 'Will, do you realize what you've just done? Today you broke your mould. Today you *really* did behave like superman. You have actually *grown into something else*. You really have, Will.' Molly sneezed. 'And I want to congratu-tu-tu—'

At this point Molly's teeth began to chatter really badly.

'OK, Molly,' said Willy. 'Let's get you inside. Before you catch pneumonia. Will these guys all, you know, stay hypnotized?'

'Do icepops stay cold in the freezer?' Molly answered.

The roof garden belonged to an enormous, flashy penthouse. This apartment was made up mainly of one long, rectangular room that was almost the same size as the footprint of the building. It had skyline views of Manhattan all around. Through the end window, the Empire State Building twinkled like a Christmas decoration. At the other end of the huge room was a high-tech, open-plan kitchen, whilst halfway along it was the sitting area with rugs and furry, sausage-shaped sofas. This is where Molly sat, with Petula on her lap and Willy at her side.

Molly had given each of the gang strict instructions. Now, as diligently as robots, they were busily cleaning the place up. Heaps of empty beer cans were being piled into black dustbin bags and the hundreds of cigarette stubs that riddled the floor like strange animal-droppings were being swept up. Choker was in an apron dusting the tops of shelves, whilst DT was hoovering and the horny-headed man was wearing pink rubber gloves and scrubbing the kitchen cupboards. The floors were being washed and the place was beginning to smell lemony-fresh. Soon they would be finished, and then, as ordered, they would leave and never return – each one of them to pursue a crime-free career. Doris was sitting in front of Molly, Petula and Willy like a good schoolgirl.

'So,' Molly interrogated. 'You're telling me that you've squatted in this apartment for six months?'

'Yeah – the owner is – this – crazy dood – who has so – much dough – he has houses – all over the world – An' like he's gone – Who knows – he may never come back.'

Molly glanced about at the oil paintings on the walls and at the ancient, limbless marble sculptures. She turned to Willy.

'Why don't you live here for a bit, Will? You can look at it as your payment for helping the owner get rid of this lot – and as your reward for catching eight Manhattan hooligans. If the owner comes back, just give me a call and I can come and sort him out.'

Willy's eyebrow slid up and down like a caterpillar walking over a stone.

'Because,' continued Molly, 'you can't live on the streets forever. Imagine how cold this winter is going to be. You'll get frostbite. Unless you like living on the street. Do you?'

'Not really.'

'See, so if you stay in this apartment for a bit, you can keep clean and warm and sort yourself out. I get paid a lot by the theatre, I can easily help you with money.' Molly was quiet for a moment. 'Just think, if you use those two sorts of hypnotism I told you about, you know, charm and self-hypnosis – 'Every day in every way I get better and better and better' – you really will go places, Will.' Molly smiled. 'It's *Will* power! I've been thinking, you see. And I reckon there are *two* domino ways of looking at life. *One way* is that life's a game of luck – that you only win dominoes in life if you're lucky. It's nice to win dominoes, but *the other way* of looking at life is seeing that it's also all about knocking dominoes over. You know – the domino effect.

'If you just sit on the street and never do anything, nothing will ever happen. You've got to do something. That will be the first domino, and that will knock the next domino and lead to something else and so on . . .' Molly paused, amazed that she was giving a grown man a pep talk. She was worried about Will's future, she realized. That was why she was doing it. Then she hit him with the big question. 'Have you any idea what work you might be able to do to start the dominoes off? You see, you've got to earn your living, Will.' Willy shifted his feet as he considered telling Molly his thoughts.

'It may look to you, Molly, like what I've been doing is nothin'. But actually I've got my first domino an' it's nearly ready to knock over. I *have* been workin'.' Molly looked surprised. 'You see, livin' on the streets, I have noticed something that I've been meaning to write to the mayor about, except I haven't had a fixed address for him to write back to. And it's kinda related to dominoes too.'

Molly nodded in encouragement. 'Go on.'

'Well, livin' on the streets for four years, you notice things. Certain things. Like if the pavin' stones are loose or at a slant you see how easy it is for people to trip. I've seen old ladies an' joggers go flyin'. You notice what happens when the streets ain't clean, especially for blind people – whoa, I once saw this blind man step in a melted ice cream an' it splat right up his trouser leg and the poor guy had no idea he'd got so sticky. I saw another man step in somethin' worse an' I felt real sorry for him. I've seen moms with strollers getting' their wheels stuck in ruts. I've seen a guy fall down a manhole an break his leg! But the thing I noticed that I think will interest the mayor is somethin' I noticed because of my love of dominoes.'

Molly sat riveted. Willy gazed out at the sky, remembering.

'One day I was looking at the layout of the pavin' stones on the sidewalk and it struck me that they weren't laid out as cleverly as they could be. I have a lotta spare dominoes and, well, I thought I'd work out whether those pavin' stones could be laid out more sensibly. An' I found that there was a big mistake in the way those slabs were distributed. Every street I camped on, I got into the habit of testing the layout of the sidewalks. An' I have found that Manhattan is using *three slabs too many* for each stretch of sidewalk. They cut them up in the wrong places and waste pavin' stones. Some Victorian dude must have set out how they get laid out, a long, long time ago and right to this day all the slab layers follow that pattern. But it's wrong. You think how much pavin' there is in New York. I could save the mayor a lotta dough if he just listened to me.'

Molly was astounded.

'Wow, it sounds like you're some sort of mathematical genius,' she said. A flush of pride reddened Willy's face.

'No genius, just a guy with time on his hands. I'm glad you like it though.'

'If I like it, just think how much the mayor will!' said Molly. 'Let's go out for dinner to celebrate. And you can write him a letter!'

The next day the real model, Maximillion Most, woke up cold and depressed on the pavement outside the Bellingham Hotel. His car was parked on the road and its keys were in his hand. He had no idea how he had spent such a grim night outside, nor how he had found himself in the stinking clothes and oilskin jacket that he was wearing. As a smart businessman walked past, and spat at him, saying, 'Get a life,' he was haunted by his own behaviour the day before.

'You have no idea!' he shouted after the businessman. 'You have no idea what I've been through. Or how cold it is on this street. Do you think I CHOSE to sleep out here?'

'Aw, get lost, loser,' the stony-faced Wall Street worker shouted back.

Max pulled himself up. His legs were so stiff from the low temperatures that he could hardly walk. He hobbled to his car and, as he slipped into its front seat, he began to cry.

The next week, Molly and Petula were back at work at the theatre. Molly was trying on her silver space costume when there was a knock at the dressing-room door.

'Mail,' the theatre caretaker said, passing her an envelope. Molly took it back to the table and settled down to read it. It was from Willy. As she opened the letter, a photograph fell out on to her lap. It was a picture of him in a black suit with irregular white spots on it.

Dear Molly

I thought you might like to see a picture of me in my new suit. The mayor loved my idea, and after I told him everything he made me 'Chief Sidewalk Inspector'. Would you believe that? My job is to keep an eye on the streets of Manhattan so they're safe an' clean. He thinks I'm goin' to save Manhattan money, since if there are no accidents there will be no people suing the city. He also thinks that in the long term my paving-stone observation is goin' to save a fortune. He's rung his mayor friends in other cities too: Chicago, Los Angeles, Washington, an' they're all keen to know more. He's bringin' them over next Tuesday an' I'll be doin' a presentation. I'm real nervous about it.

Every so often I sit still and think how much is happenin' so quickly and it feels like a dream. I'm knockin' over dominoes so fast I can't keep up any more. Who knows, maybe every city in America will soon have a Chief Sidewalk Inspector.

I wanted to thank you, Molly, for helpin' me push the first domino over. If it weren't for you, I'd still be camping.

You know where I am. Give me a call, or maybe we'll just bump into each other on the sidewalk.

Keep linin' those dominoes up!

Yours truly,
William Dumfry

Molly spun around to look for Petula. There on the floor were eight empty sacks – the sacks for the scores of dominoes that Willy had given her. Their contents were lined up on the floor, like black-and-white figures in a queue.

Petula sat at the start place. She cocked her head to one side and whined beseechingly. Molly leaned back against her swivel chair, crossed her right leg over her left and folded her arms. Then she smiled.

'OK, Petula, go for it.'

The little dog raised her paw and gently nudged the first domino. And the curling wand of two hundred dominoes clicked and clacked their way around the room.

The
Chill-Out Pack
Contains:

- 1 mini TV
- 1 radio/CD player
- 1 inflatable armchair
- 1 pirate snuggle bag
- 1 lava lamp
- loads of books and magazines

See the back cover of this book for
how to enter this competition.

For postcard entries send your card to:
Molly Moon Competition
Macmillan Children's Books
Pan Macmillan Publishers
20 New Wharf Road
London N1 9RR